Wacky Quack

WACKY
QUACK
QUACK, HONK!
My First
SHARED READING
Preller Geldenhuys

Dedication

Preston Gray Chellew

This is a Book 1 (See last page for

parents and Book grades)

The Beginning

In the beginning, God created

all the ducks – White ones,

brown ones, multi-coloured

ones – all sorts of colours.

Wacky Quack was born at

Beulah, Paeroa – right in the

middle of everywhere in New

Zealand.

It was a land of milk and honey

for ducks of every kind.

Beulah had everything that

ducks and geese liked.

It had green grasslands,

stream and ponds, and even

generous quantities of grain-

food – the sort that ducks

loved.

Wacky Quack was a real

greedy duck.

Just like his friend Wonky

Honkey

They fought for their food.

He quickly learned that the

white ducks were very noisy

and would not come too close

to Pakehas.

And not at all like his good

friend Wonky Honkey.

Birds can sing songs!

Just like parrots – see the Youtube that went viral.

YouTube

My Sunshine

This book

My Sunshine is 76 years old today.

Beulah Stories

Behind
The Pictures

YOU ARE
MY
SUNSHINE

MY ONLY SUNSHINE

YOU MAKE
ME HAPPY

WHEN SKIES
ARE GRAY

YOU'LL NEVER KNOW

DEAR, HOW MUCH
I LOVE YOU

Dee and Preller Geldenhuys

Sing my favourite song

you are my sunshine

You are my Sunshine,

my only sunshine

You are my SUNSHINE
MY ONLY YOU MAKE ME
SUNSHINE HAPPY
when skies are grey

You make my happy

When skies are grey

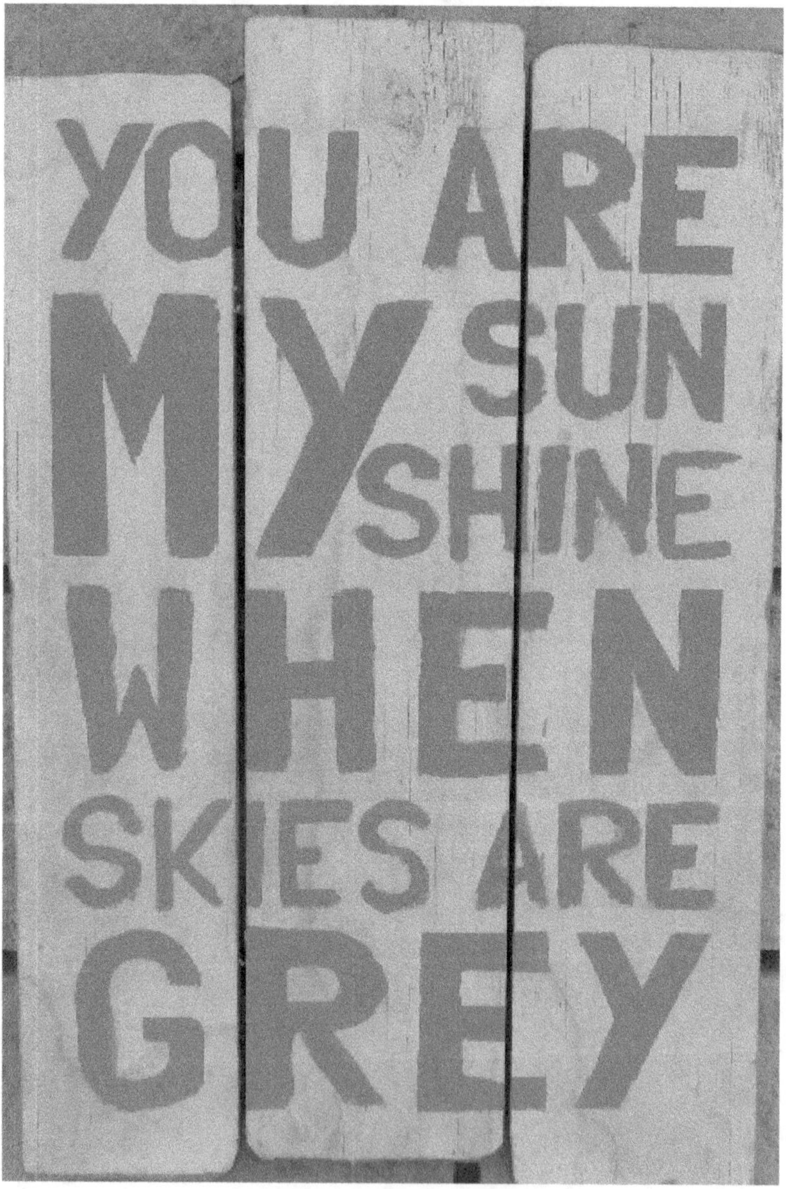

YOU ARE
MY SUN
SHINE
WHEN
SKIES ARE
GREY

You never know, dear

How much I love you.

So please don't take my

Sunshine Away.

(Sung to Gogga at 2:20am on

her birthday)

Difficulty

I can spell 'difficulty' –

Mr D, Mr I, Mr FFI,

Mr C, Mr U, Mr LTY

= D I FF I C U LT Y

Acknowledgements

Preston Gray

Preston Grey Chellew is the authors first great-grandchild.

He deserves the best

opportunity to read and write,

do arithmetic and master

calculus.

Oumie (Nana) for line

drawings.

Anne Oliver for some of the

illustrations

Wonky Honky - https://www.amazon.com/dp/B08X
P9JTYR

Beulah Series –

Beulah Places - https://www.amazon.com/dp/B08L
1QD8SW

Other Books

Little Red Riding Hood

Based on the story by The Brothers Grimm

Illustrated by Mike Gordon

Little Red Riding Hood was one of my first fairy tales of my Grimm Brother's books that parents my gave me.

The brothers were born during the 1780s in Hanau, Germany and studied law at Marburg University. After leaving education, they worked as diplomats and librarians in

Kassel.

In 1837 they were dismissed

from their professorships at the

University of Göttingen for

refusing to swear allegiance to

the new King of Hanover, but

were later invited to join the

Academy in Berlin, by

Frederick William IV of Prussia.

They remained there for the rest of their lives. Individually and as a team the brothers were two of the great scholars that Germany has produced Wilhelm died in 1859 at age 73 and Jacob died in 1863 at age 78.

Grimms' Fairy Tales

❖ ❖ ❖ ❖ ❖

J.L.C. & W.C. GRIMM

Goldilocks and the Three Bears

Retold by
Susanna Davidson
Illustrated by Mike Gordon

Goldilocks
and the
Three Bears

Retold by Susanna Davidson
Narrated by Lesley Sims

Illustrated by Mike Gordon

Reading Consultant: Alison Kelly

USBORNE FIRST READING

The Hare and the Tortoise

Retold by
Mairi Mackinnon

Illustrated by
Daniel Howarth

The Story of
Black Beauty
with AUDIO
Illustrated by
Alan Marks

Cat and the Beanstalk

Jack and the Beanstalk

Cinderella

Snow White (and the seven dwarfs)

Hansel and Gretel

Sleeping Beauty

Rapunzel

Aladdin and the Lamp

I Love My Dog
by
Angela Smith
PROUD SUPPORTER
PAW JUSTICE

i LoVe You
BooK
by
Libby
Hathorn
illustrated by
Heath
M<Kenzie

"My hope is that Wonky's strong spirit will inspire people of all ages to believe in themselves, no matter what life brings"

Lazy Daisy, Busy Lizzie
Mary Ellen Jordan & Andrew Weldon
PDF

Lazy Daisy, Busy Lizzie

Mary Ellen Jordan
& Andrew Weldon

Peppa Pig Stories

Oink
oink !

Meow
meow!

Peppa Pig
Peppa's Summer Holiday

Peppa's summer holiday to the coast.

The family travel to the airport

They quickly showed their passports

They showed their passports
and tickets

The air hostess showed them
to their seats

Daddy saw the sea, Mummy pig noticed the palm trees but Peppa pig liked the swimming pool

Daddy Pig jumped into the pool

Miss Rabbit arrived at the pool
...de an announcement.
...on please! This afternoon's holiday
...is a visit to a turtle sanctuary."
"Oooh!" gasped children.
"If turtle hatchlings are being rel...
the sea today, we may be able to...
from a distance," said Miss Rabbit.

Peppa pig meets her friends.

They ask Mummy to go to the pool.

Splash! Splash!

The next day, Peppa and George went straight to the pool.
"Suzy! Zoe!" cried Peppa. "What are YOU doing here?"
"We're on holiday!" replied Suzy Sheep and Zoe Zebra.

After the jungle trip, everyone jumped into the pool.
"Our last holiday activity is a dance competition," said Miss Rabbit, "in the swimming pool!"
Peppa was very excited and started to dance.
"Look at me – I'm doing a flamingo dance!" she cried.
The children laughed and copied Peppa's funny flamingo dance.
Hee!
Hee!
Hee!
Hee!

Peppa pig sits in front of his
mother.

Her brother sits in front of his father.

Everyone **loved** their summer holiday, and **everyone** loved Peppa's flamingo dance!

Every one loved their holiday.

It was hot in the jungle.

Peppa wanted one last swim.

George enjoys swimming too!

Splash!

George enjoys
swimming!

Adult advice

Encourage your children to read books and take them to your local library at soon as possible – to choose their own books to read at their leisure.

Book Grading

 Ideal for sharing with emergent readers

 Simple sentences for eager new readers

 High-interest stories for developing readers

 Complex plots for confident readers

 The perfect bridge to chapter books

**For more information about the
I Can Read Book® series, see inside!**

1 = Yellow + Blue – Babies

2 = Red - Age 3 to 5 years

3 = Green – complex plots

4 = Purple – Chapter books

Cover design: Peysoft Publishing
Illustrations: Rina Geldenhuys and
Anne Olivier

ISBN: 979-873286443-4
ePub:

Other books in this Series: -

Wonky Honkey
Wacky Quack
Two Tongue
Red Riding Hood
Peppa Pig